Simon Says

By Nanette Kryske Towsley

Simon Says

A True Story by Nanette Kryske Towsley

To Markie
My Co-Director of the
Towsley Pet Ranch & Spa
With Love.

HELLO. MY NAME IS SIMON.
I AM A DESERT COTTONTAIL RABBIT,
BORN AT A RANCH IN CAVE CREEK, ARIZONA.

It is a magical place with bunnies everywhere and lots of horses to play around. It is easy to live in harmony with the people and even the dogs here. We just do our thing, and they do theirs. Sometimes we are even super close. But no one chooses to break that "personal space" boundary.

BUNNIES EVERYWHERE!

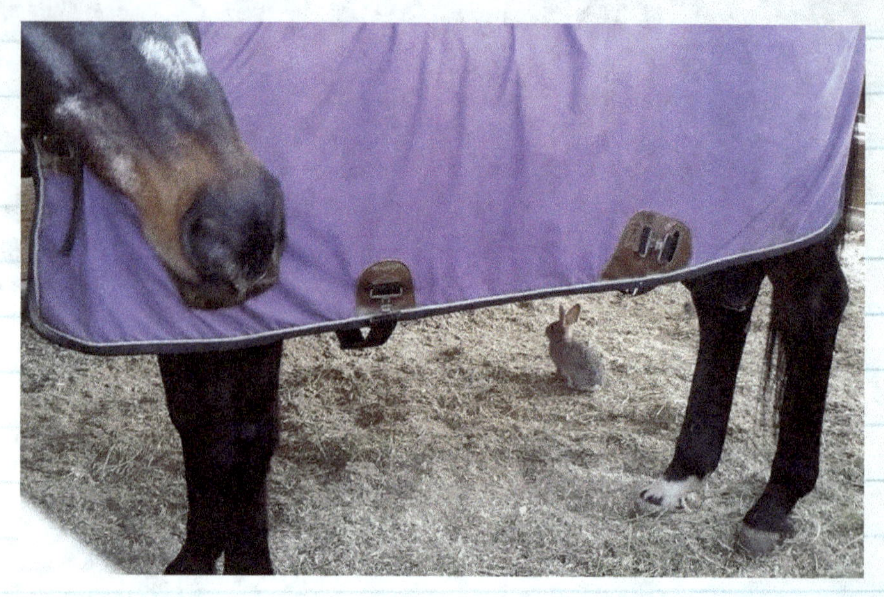

HORSES ARE A PERFECT PLACE FOR BUNNIES TO HIDE!

My birth was a normal bunny birth-smooshed into a little nest with my siblings. Momma would come once or twice a day when no one was around. She didn't want to attract attention to any of the many hawks, coyotes, cats, snakes, or other predators who would think we were a fine snack.

Being the little adventurous bunny of the bunch, every family has one, I took to the shavings like hoomans take to the streets.

Unfortunately, like my hooman counterparts, I was very unprepared for what I would encounter.

But I found a warm, safe, dry spot. It was the beginning of February and it was going to be almost freezing this night. I could stay in the warm nest with my brother and sister, or I could find something more suitable. After a few attempts, I found the perfect spot. Under a big, warm horse. He blocked the wind and his body heat gave off a comfortable temperature on the cold night that was descending.

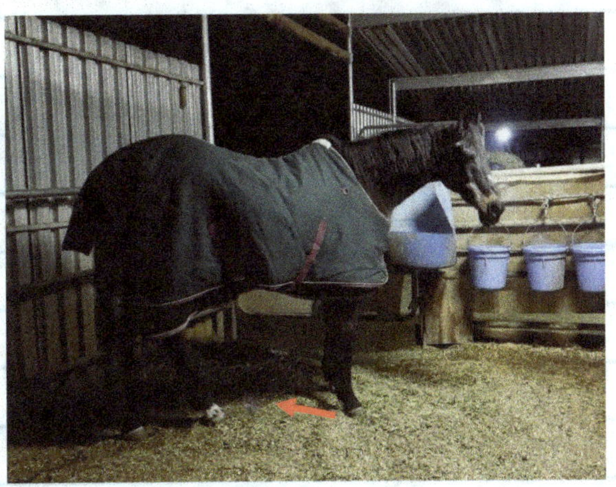

The horse, Woody, didn't move much since he was focused on his dinnertime feed in his feeder. He would drop grain out of his mouth, so I made a note for when I am able to eat solid food. I'm pretty sure that is why Momma picked this place since it was a good food source. Woody was old. Not just kinda old, but like 38 years old. Which makes him like 115 in hooman years, and God knows what in rabbit years. Either way, I found him a perfect source of comfort this February night.

Then in a flash, before I knew it, Woody's hooman was in the stall adjusting his cold weather blanket, and she not only spied me there by his big foot, she picked me up. I don't think she realized what she had found at first. Then she muttered something about "well that's not a very safe place for a baby like you. Right next to the big Woodster's hoof!"

I was kind of in shock since I wasn't expecting to deal with this on my third day of life. Next thing I knew this hooman put me in a white bucket filled with hay and I went for a ride somewhere. I knew my Mom would be upset, but I needed to focus on what was coming next. Clearly, I had no one to talk to about it.

MY NEW ADVENTURE HAD BEGUN.

Oh my gosh, she picked me up and held me in her warm, gentle hand. At first, I wasn't quite sure what she was going to do. I hadn't heard of people who ate bunny rabbit in our part of the country, so I figured that was off the table. For now, at least.

She never hurt me, just handled me carefully and asked what I preferred to eat. That was a lot cooler than my Bunny Momma since she never asked. She just forced it on me. Wow, at this stage of my early life, I was given a choice. I could get to like this. I was obviously not a normal bunny.

I was indeed a very lucky bunny. With opportunities abounding, thought this would be a perfect time to play along and see what comes of it. So instead of being scared and worried, I relaxed and enjoyed the mere comfort of this kind hooman who took interest in me. I just sat in her hand without squirming or trying to get away.

I HAD NO BETTER PLACE TO GO AT THIS POINT ANYWAY.

On my first day or so, I spent a lot of
time in my little white bucket with hay
in it. It was pretty close to the nest
where I was born, so I had no reason to
hunt for another place. My hooman put
a little dish with water in one side of it.
After I took a sip, I found it kind of fun to
sit in it, water and all. Every time I did
that, she would take it out, pick me up,
dry me off, and put in a the cup replaced
with water again. I figured I had to learn
something from this process, because it
happened many times.

Being the smart baby bunny, I caught on, but on the other paw, I found it fun to keep playing in it. The hay was also kind of tasty, but she was convinced I still needed baby formula. So she took this small little tube with slightly warm kitten milk in it, and I raced for it.

Just like my Bunny Momma made, except for kitties. I would drink the whole tube. She didn't get a lot of photos of that since when she held me and the food tube, she had no hands for her camera phone. She was slick, but not that slick.

After all, she didn't know if I was going to squirm or jump out or run away. I knew I wasn't, but she was worried her dogs would make me nervous and do something stupid. But I was a quick study, and figured out that the more I played along, the more freedom I would ultimately have.

SO WE STARTED BUILDING THIS AMAZING FRIENDSHIP.

I became the cute, cuddly bunny
she was hoping for, and she was
kind, gentle, and loving. A
perfect combination. She took
me out anytime I scratched on
the white bucket. That was my
secret language and she was
pretty quick too and caught on. I
could really get to like this.

Next thing I knew, she had found a really
cool glass home for me. It was big and had
hiding places for me, spots for food and
water, and what I guessed was a place to
go potty. In the barn, we could go
anywhere, but I knew that it would help
my cause if I was respectful and used what
she thought of as a kitty-litter box. We
both played off of each other's cleverness
and hopefulness.

My glass home was large and fresh and light from the sunny window. I was placed on a counter in her home near a lot of activity. Her fellow hooman was a jolly big guy with white hair and fur on his face like mine. He would come and peer in at me and use soft, deep words to comfort me. I think he was afraid to hold me, so instead he would watch and talk to me. He probably didn't know what to do if I squirmed or squiggled my way out of his big hands.

WE ALL GOT ALONG FAMOUSLY.

I behaved. They behaved. And life was good. Days
would go by, and my hooman would give me the
tube of warm kitten milk that I kept drinking,
making me stronger and healthier

After a few days, my hooman started carrying my glass home into her car, taking me for a 15-minute ride to her office. She worked at a church and everyone was super nice and kind there. My home sat on the corner of her office desk. Then, I met lots of new people. Some wanted to hold me, some just stared in disbelief. I was good with all of it. They all took selfies with me. I just sat there looking cute. Seemed to work to keep them happy. I was truly feeling safe and comfortable with my hooman and my new glass home.

Here's me in a Subaru-whatever that is.

I even got to be let out
and run on the big
floor in another office.
It was still lots of fun
even though there
were not a lot of cool
hiding places like my
hooman's office with
lots of junk everywhere
to sneak into.

I'm not quite sure what "hide and seek" is.

Hoomans are funny. They automatically assume their kindness is not enough. They give us little creatures other little animal friends, thinking we will feel comforted. I am not complaining, but my hooman companionship was totally fulfilling, especially since I was never left alone for long. But I hung out with my stuffed squirrel, humoring my people so they would continue to think of me as a good bunny. As long as I appeared happy, they were content as well.

They would watch me through my glass windows.
When my hooman noticed I was eating the
delicious food she gave me, she figured I didn't
need that warm milk anymore. She was right, but I
liked that stuff. It reminded me of my Bunny
Momma and it kind of made me sad. Wondering
what I was missing as a regular bunny that never
left the barn. Maybe someday I would find out.
Who knows?

In a very short time, I noticed my little poofy white tail started to grow. So did my ears. I was thriving actually. Good food, love, warm comfort, and the familiar sights and smells of my environment at both my hooman's home and in her office - I was doing great. I had no idea how long I had been there, somedays seemed like it was yesterday. Other days, it seemed like a long time from the shavings in the stall.

It was pretty darn clear, no one was going to hurt me, and they all cared for me deeply. They always would get a big smile on their face when they approached my cage. That look was not wasted on me. I tried to smile back in my own little bunny way. Hoomans should try that on themselves, maybe they would have a better world if they spent more time doing that. What do I know, I am a little bunny, not a sociologist.

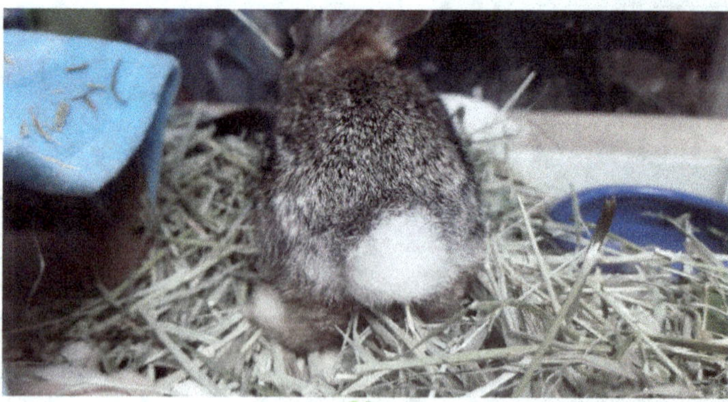

Score

Hoomans are funny. They automatically assume their kindness is not enough. They give us little creatures other little animal friends, thinking we will feel comforted. I am not complaining, but my hooman companionship was totally fulfilling, especially since I was never left alone for long. But I hung out with my stuffed squirrel, humoring my people so they would continue to think of me as a good bunny. As long as I appeared happy, they were content as well.

My hooman was pretty smart on the needs of baby
bunnies. She must have "Googled" what to do.
Although most of the time, the stories said
something about never touching a wild animal. I
heard her on the telephone explaining to people
that I surely would have been dead if staying in
what I thought was a great place under Woody.
Apparently, Woody had big feet that he was not
always conscious of where he put them, and if I
wasn't careful I would find myself under the hoof of
a 1,000-pound horse. That could not be good, so I
guess she had no other choice. I know she looked
for my nest, but when she didn't find it, she made
the executive decision to save my life. She kept
telling me that soon it would be my choice. If I
wanted to stay a pet or be returned to my home as
a strong, healthy bunny able to fend for myself. I
was digging this, so I wasn't ready for anything
other what I was doing.

I loved my outside habitat, created just for me. Some cagey thing with lots of room for me to run and play outside in the sunshine of the day with real leaves and sticks. My hooman tossed in a water bowl and some fresh hay to munch, in case I got hungry on the road. So much fun. Again, I could feel the heart behind what my hooman was doing for me, helping me to be the best bunny I could be.

I got to explore from
this outdoor heaven,
just about everyday. It
made me feel like a
"Natural Bunny."

I really got to stretch my legs and hop. It felt so good.

I even had little tiny dumbbells made from Timothy hay. You could munch on them after you did sets of deadlifts and curls.

My life was really settling in. I enjoyed sitting in my food bowls on occasion- just a comfort to remind me of how safe and supported I felt. Always a smorgasbord of greens, bowls of pellets and good nutrients, fresh water, and occasional treats of carrots and apples. And I mean occasional.

Urban legend alert! Everyone thinks bunnies live on carrots. Well, I am here to tell you we love them. But if we ate them in any quantity, we would end up diabetic. Yes, diabetic. They and most fruits have too much sugar. So in moderation, like anything, they are fine. But don't go too crazy no matter how tasty they are. You need to think of your life in years to come and pay off from your behavior when you are young.

I learned about holidays. Happy Valentine's Day!

Easter is all about bunnies. And Jesus too.

My hooman took me in the shower. Not to get a bath, but to let me run and play. And she sat in there with me. It was super fun to be loose and free to explore in the house. I heard the doggies outside the door wanting to get in. I was safe and didn't worry.

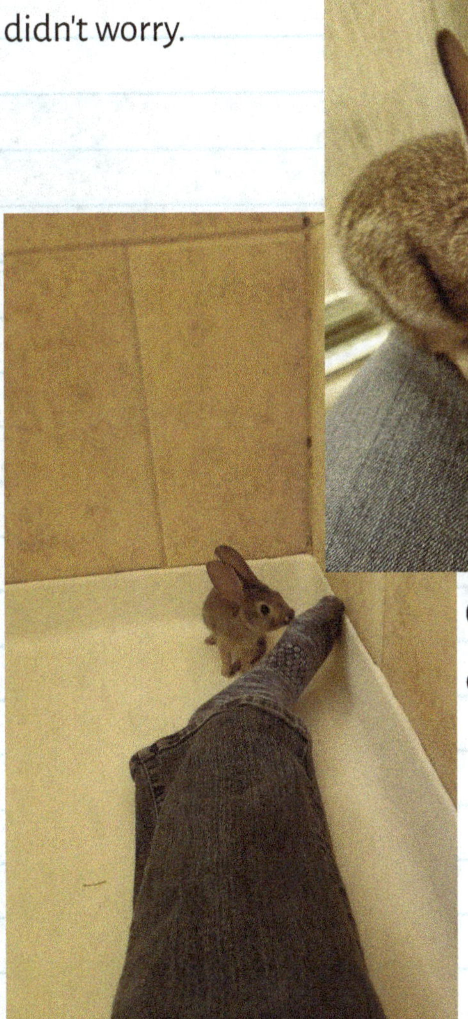

Check out how my ears have grown!

We ate breakfast together.

Nothing better than a lunch of kale with a

tinge of parsley.

I was now becoming a big boy bunny.

I was healthy, growing, and starting to feel

my, well, wild oats.

43

I could feel I was changing. Along with my ears
growing, so were my little bunny hormones. It was
late March now, and now matter how much I loved
this special charmed life, I realized this was not the
life I was meant to lead. I needed to tell my
Hooman Mom that it was time. I didn't want to
hurt her feelings for all that she had done for me,
but I know she would want to know the truth. She
always told me I would have the ultimate choice.

But my hooman is super intuitive especially with animals. She knew it was time to let me go. Time to go be the bunny she raised me to be.

HAPPY, HEALTHY, AND FREE.

I needed the companionship of other bunnies and the risks of life I was meant to experience. So on March 29th, her wedding anniversary with the big guy with the white hair and beard, they drove me back to the barn where I came from. She carefully found a safe place to say goodbye where she could let me hop off to my future.

It would not be as safe and comfortable as my hooman home, but it was the future I was meant to have. We all knew it. Letting go and saying goodbye are as much a part of life, as anything else.

Sadness should be replaced by love and memories. It is for parents letting go of children, children letting go of their parents, people with their pets, friends letting friends move on to greater adventures. It is always a tough moment but something life requires. From it comes growth and hope. And God watches over us in our new directions, as He did all along.

But I must say at this particular moment in my little bunny life, and that of my hooman Mom's, it really sucked. But I know in my little bunny heart, I need to do this. And Mom knew too.

She gently placed me down in the hay pile loaded with bales of both alfalfa and grass hay. She put some of my favorite kale in as a last offering. A low horse feed bucket was place nearby with fresh water, that she continued to filled every day for the next 9 months. Making sure I found my own sources of food and water. I knew I was up to the task. It was inside me all along. But now that I had my full health, as a more mature bunny, I could fend for myself much better. Especially better than if Woody the horse squished me on that night in early February.

GREAT HIDING PLACES.

SO MUCH SPACE!

AND FRIENDS!

Wow, other bunnies to run and play, and nibble on hay with. I wonder where my siblings are?

I hung out daily where my hooman Mom could find me and see that I was fine. I would hear her call my name, like she always would. "Simon, Simon, how's my little boy." She knew it was me, although we all looked a like. I would twitch my ears when she called so she knew I recognized my name being called. Also, when she came after me with her camera phone, I knew it was her and posed.

I got some of the others to do that as well, but most of them thought the selfie and camera phone thing was freaky. But I would hang around so she knew it was me.

Days would come and go. I cavorted with my bunny pals. We ate from the plentiful supply and the puddles of water. And Mom's water bucket.

Life is good for all of us. We all have that life experience in us. Behind us. Walking into the next adventure. For me, finding a companion and having my own babies.

Maybe Mom will rescue one of those some cold night in winter and return her or him to the wild when it is time. Or not.

No one knows what future lies ahead. But as those hooman philosophers say, live it one day at a time, and make the most of each and every day. Hard to know when one of those will be our last.

LIFE. WOW. LIVE IT. LOVE IT.

Still here. In person and in our hearts. There is always room for "hop" and joy. OK, no more silly bunny puns, hope and joy.
To my dear reader for hanging on this long, what's your next adventure?

LIFE LESSONS
CAN COME FROM
THE LITTLEST OF CREATURES
IN THE STRANGEST WAYS.

Moreover, they can influence people at any age. The themes of giving care, experiencing nature, taking chances, and letting go have timeless value even when provided by a little bunny. *Simon Says* is a heart-warming story with a message of love.

NANETTE KRYSKE TOWSLEY

has spent a lifetime in advertising, marketing, and communications. She originally hails from the Westside of Los Angeles, but now resides in Phoenix, Arizona with her husband of several decades and a myriad of rescued pets.

If you enjoyed this book, please check out, "Little Birds of A Feather" — her first book that is a photographic journey of two abandoned, baby, wild birds' rescue and release back to the wild.

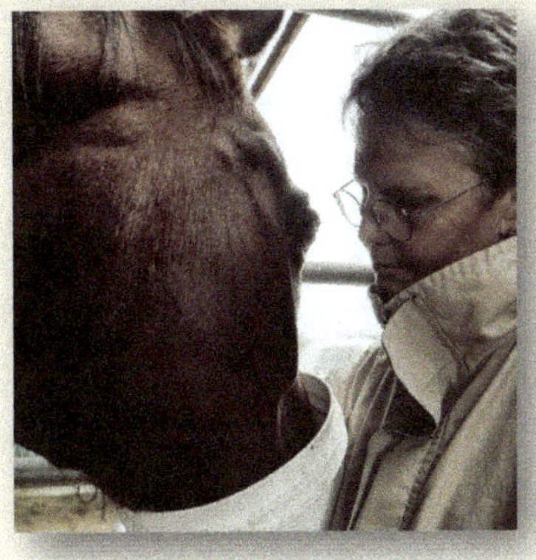